This is a story about new beginnings and hope.
The seeds and words which are sown today bear fruit tomorrow.

Pauline Stewart

To Leila who first said 'Nothing happened'.
PS

For my mother and her granddaughter Eloise.
NM

1 3 5 7 9 10 8 6 4 2

Text copyright © Pauline Stewart 2000
Illustrations copyright © Nick Maland 2000

Pauline Stewart and Nick Maland have asserted their rights under the
Copyright, Designs and Patents Act, 1988, to be identified as the author
and illustrator of this work

First published in the United Kingdom 2000
by The Bodley Head Children's Books
Random House, 20 Vauxhall Bridge Road, London SW1V 2SA

The Random House Group Limited Reg. No. 954009
www.randomhouse.co.uk

A CIP catalogue record for this book
is available from the British Library

ISBN 0 370 32459 5

Printed in Hong Kong by Midas Printing Ltd

SUNSHINE SHOWERS
AND FOUR O'CLOCK FLOWERS

PAULINE STEWART AND NICK MALAND

THE BODLEY HEAD
LONDON

The earth was wet and claggy.
'Go on,' said Grandma Ernestine,
'...pop in the seed.'

Davina couldn't wait. She dropped
the seed into the mud by the shed
and patted the ground with her spade.
  'What's going to happen, Grandma?'
she asked with excitement.

'Oh, something special I should think.
You may get Jack up his beanstalk.

'Or a weird and wonderful monkey puzzle tree.
You'll just have to wait and see.'

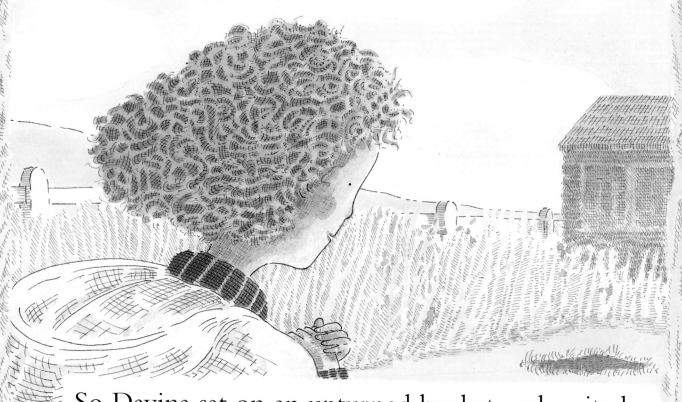

So Davina sat on an upturned bucket and waited.

She waited until the cows came home.

While she waited, Davina did cartwheels, handstands and jumping jacks.

Then she sank into the tall grass in front of the four o'clock flowers.

She waited until the golden sun
went to bed in the west.

She waited until the moon shone
weakly and the stars showed off.
'Plants need light,' she said as she turned on
her torch and buttoned up her coat.

'Come inside,' said Grandma Ernestine. She gave Davina a hug. She knew how lonely Davina was. 'Go on with you now,' she said, 'and don't worry, sometimes magic happens when you're not looking.'

Davina dragged her heels along the garden
path and slowly climbed the back steps.

Grandma Ernestine was thoughtful
as she put on her hairnet for bed.

Spring came but
nothing had sprung.

'I know,' said Grandma Ernestine
one weekend, 'perhaps it needs a little
encouragement. Let's sing to it.'

So they did. They sang:
'All things bright and beautiful,
All flowers good and small.
All things new and wonderful,
Just let them grow, that's all.'

It rained.
'That's good,' said Grandma Ernestine. It didn't feel good to Davina – but then something did happen.

The rain stopped. There was a knock on the door.
'Hello,' said the children, 'can we play with you?'

Davina played with her new friends. They took
great care not to squash anything.

Her friends came again and again.
There was still no Jack up his beanstalk.
There was still no weird and wonderful
monkey puzzle tree.
    But something was beginning to grow.

And Davina wasn't lonely any more.

As the seedling grew into a tree, and the tree grew tall and strong, so did Davina.

Grandma Ernestine was old now.
'In time,' she said, 'a seed will always grow.
And when it starts, there is no stopping it.

'There's a beginning,

and a middle...

'...and no end.'

Davina held the seeds which
would start a new story and smiled.

Grandma Ernestine had been right.